MR MONKEY

AND THE BIRTHDAY PARTY

There are lots of Early Reader stories
you might enjoy.

Look at the back of the book or,
for a complete list, visit
www.orionbooks.co.uk

MR MONKEY

AND THE BIRTHDAY PARTY

Linda Chapman

Illustrated by Sam Hearn

Orion
Children's Books

First published in Great Britain in 2014
by Orion Children's Books
a division of the Orion Publishing Group Ltd
Orion House
5 Upper Saint Martin's Lane
London WC2H 9EA
An Hachette UK Company

1 3 5 7 9 10 8 6 4 2

Text © Linda Chapman 2014
Illustrations © Sam Hearn 2014

ISBN 978 1 4440 0985 9

To Spike and his best friends,
Seb, Alfie and Oscar. I hope you enjoy
Mr Monkey's adventures!

Contents

Chapter One

This is Mr Monkey.

He looks like any other cuddly
toy. But Mr Monkey is magic –
yes, magic!

Mr Monkey belongs to Class Two. The children don't know he's magic, but when Mr Monkey is around, exciting things always start to happen.

On Monday morning, Miss Preston took Mr Monkey off the shelf. "Now, Class Two, before we have our story, it's time to decide who will take Mr Monkey home this week. Whoever takes him must write a diary about all the things you do together."

The children sat up straight
and looked hopeful.

Miss Preston smiled at a girl in the front. "Anya, why don't you look after Mr Monkey?"

"Thank you, Miss!" Anya had just started at the school. She felt very special being chosen.

Mr Monkey winked at her.

Anya jumped. "Miss!"

"What is it, Anya?" Miss Preston said.

Anya didn't reply. Mr Monkey had definitely winked at her. He had!

"Are you OK, Anya?" Miss Preston said.

Anya realised everyone was staring. "Um… yes, sorry, Miss."

Mr Monkey looked just like a normal toy now. She must have imagined it. She sat down to listen to the story with the rest of the class.

Chapter Two

At going-home-time, the class put their chairs on the desks.

"It's my birthday party tomorrow, Miss," said Rachel. "I'm having a swimming party."

"I'll look forward to hearing all about it," said Miss Preston. "Good afternoon, everybody."

"Good afternoon, Miss Preston," the class said. Then they all rushed for the door.

Anya put Mr Monkey carefully on the bench while she put on her outdoor shoes.

"I can't wait till your party!"
Martha said to Rachel.

"It's going to be brilliant," said
Rachel. "It won't be a babyish
party where we have to stay in
the little pool. Everyone who can
swim is allowed in the big pool!"

Anya froze.

"I'm glad we can all swim,"
said Maddy.

Rachel nodded. "See you
tomorrow!"

Anya felt sick. "Oh, Mr Monkey," she whispered. "I can't swim at all. What am I going to do?"

Chapter Three

Anya thought about the party all the way home. If she couldn't go in the big pool, everyone would laugh at her. Maybe she could pretend to be sick? But then she would miss the party.

When they got back, Anya sat on the sofa and buried her face in her hands. "I don't know what to do," she whispered.

Suddenly Mr Monkey sat up. "Maybe I can help," he said.

Anya jumped to her feet with a squeak.

Mr Monkey blinked at her. "Hello, Anya!"

"You're… you're alive!" Anya couldn't believe it. She shut her eyes and opened them again.

"Boo!" said Mr Monkey.

Anya cried out.

Mr Monkey grinned. "Yes I am! And, luckily for you, I am a **genius** at solving problems. So, you can't swim very well?"

"N. . . no." Anya thought she must be in a dream. "I always sink if I try to swim without armbands. I think I'm going to pretend to be ill so I don't have to go to the party."

"You can't do that!" Mr Monkey said. "I shall get you there. But how? Hmmmm. . . I need jam!" he said suddenly.

"Jam?" said Anya.

Mr Monkey nodded. "Jam is the best thing in the world for making a brain work."

While Anya went to fetch the jam, Mr Monkey explored the room.

He looked inside the cupboards,

jumped on the sofas,

and turned the lights on and off
very quickly over and over again.

When Anya came back with
a pot of strawberry jam, Mr
Monkey ate three big spoonfuls.

"Ah, yes, this is helping!"
he said. "My brain is whizzing
faster than a hamster wheel. But
we'd better go somewhere else.
Grown ups must never find out
that I'm magic."

"We could go to my bedroom?" Anya said.

"Excellent plan!" Mr Monkey cried. "Lead the way!"

Chapter Four

Anya's favourite Dancing Dolphins playset was in the middle of her bedroom floor.

"Dolphins, hey?" Mr Monkey said.

"I wish I could swim like a dolphin," Anya sighed. "I don't know what I am going to do. . ." She stopped. Mr Monkey was jumping up and down very fast, his ears waggling. "Are you OK, Mr Monkey?"

"OK?" said Mr Monkey. "I am a hundred times **more** than OK." He beamed and spun round. "Anya, I have had an incredibly brilliant idea! Go to sleep as normal tonight and I'll solve your problem. Just wait and see!"

At midnight, Anya woke with a start. Mr Monkey was jumping on her chest.

"Wake up! It's time for your swimming lesson," he said.

"It's the middle of the night, Mr Monkey," said Anya. "I can't go outside now."

"Who said anything about outside? You're going to have a swimming lesson right here. Let the **monkey business…**" Mr Monkey flicked his tail. "…begin!"

Sparkles filled the room.
"Oh, wow!" Anya gasped.
Her playset was coming to life!

"You wished you could swim like a dolphin – well, who better to teach you?" Mr Monkey said. He waved his tail at Anya and she started to shrink.

"Hi, Anya," whistled one of the dolphins. "I'm Silver and that's Flicker."

"H. . . hello!" Anya gasped.

"It's lovely to talk to you at last," said Flicker.

"Dolphins, we really need your help. Can you teach Anya how to swim?" Mr Monkey said.

Silver and Flicker bobbed their heads. "We'd love to!" they said.

Chapter Five

"Come and play with us, Anya," Silver called.

Anya stepped into the water. It was sparkling with a golden light.

"Hold onto me and I'll pull you around," said Silver.

Anya was nervous, but she took Silver's fin and let him pull her gently through the water. Flicker swam alongside.

The two dolphins got faster and faster. Anya forgot about feeling scared and she giggled as the water sprayed up. It was so much fun!

"Look how well you're
doing!" cried Mr Monkey.
"Those dolphins will teach you
to swim in less time than it takes
a chimp to eat a banana!"

"Why don't you try swimming
underwater?" said Flicker. "It's
much easier."

Anya took a big breath and held onto Flicker as he took her underneath the water.

Suddenly he wriggled away. Anya's feet kicked and her arms moved and she carried on without him!

Anya and the dolphins swam and played chase. Flicker and Silver let Anya sit on their backs. She fell off a lot but she didn't mind.

"I love swimming!" Anya said, as she finally climbed back onto the rocks. "Thank you so much for teaching me," she said to Flicker and Silver. "I'm not worried about the party any more."

"It's been brilliant swimming together," said Silver.

"I'll never forget tonight," said Anya happily.

"Neither will we!" whistled Flicker.

"It's time to say goodbye now," Mr Monkey said. "You need to go to bed, Anya, or you'll be as sleepy as a sloth at the party. And sloths are **seriously** sleepy!"

Mr Monkey flicked his tail one more time, and Anya was back to her normal size again.

Anya looked down at her playset. The dolphins were plastic again too. "Good night, Silver," she whispered. "Good night, Flicker."

Hugging Mr Monkey tightly, Anya got into bed and went to sleep.

Chapter Six

The next day, Anya went to Rachel's swimming party. She didn't need to wear her armbands, and she even won a prize for being able to swim underwater the furthest!

Mr Monkey watched from a
chair at the side of the pool.

Everyone clapped as Anya
collected her prize. She didn't
stop smiling all the way home.

When they got back, Anya took Mr Monkey up to her bedroom. She had bought him a whole jar of strawberry jam with her pocket money.

He ate it while she thought about her diary entry. What would she write? There was so much she wanted to say.

"Can I write that you like jam?" Anya asked.

"Of course," Mr Monkey said.

Anya wrote a few lines and then smiled. "I'm really glad you're our class toy, Mr Monkey."

Mr Monkey scooped up another spoonful of jam. "You know something?" he said. "So am I!"

Mr Monkey and me went to
Rachel's party. I swam lots.
Mr Monkey didn't.

Mr Monkey ate
lots of jam.'

What are you going to read next?

More adventures with

Horrid Henry,

or go exploring with

Shumba,

and brave the Jungle

and Arctic

with Algy.

Find a frog prince with Tulsa

or even a big, yellow, whiskery

Lion in the Meadow!

Tuck into some

Blood and Guts and
Rats' Tail Pizza,

learn to dance with
Sophie,

travel back
in time with

Cudweed

and sail away in

Noah's Ark.

Enjoy all the Early Readers.